E. W. Hyde

Skew Arches

E. W. Hyde

Skew Arches

Reprint of the original, first published in 1875.

1st Edition 2024 | ISBN: 978-3-38525-149-6

Verlag (Publisher): Outlook Verlag GmbH, Zeilweg 44, 60439 Frankfurt, Deutschland
Vertretungsberechtigt (Authorized to represent): E. Roepke, Zeilweg 44, 60439 Frankfurt, Deutschland
Druck (Print): Books on Demand GmbH, In de Tarpen 42, 22848 Norderstedt, Deutschland

SKEW ARCHES.

ADVANTAGES AND DISADVANTAGES

DIFFERENT METHODS

OF CONSTRUCTION.

BY

E. W. HYDE, C.E.

NEW YORK:

D. VAN NOSTRAND, PUBLISHER,

23 MURRAY STREET AND 27 WARREN STREET.

1875.

PREFACE.

THE author was led to make the investigations contained in this little treatise by a desire to satisfy his own mind as to the relative advantages of several different methods which have been employed in the construction of Skew Arches.

The two important points of comparison that naturally suggest themselves to the investigator are:

1st. Relative security;

2d. Relative facility of construction.

A discussion and comparison of three modes of construction, with special reference to these points, will be found in the following pages, together with brief descriptions of the manner of making the necessary draughts, patterns, templets, etc.

The paper first appeared in VAN NOSTRAND'S ENGINEERING MAGAZINE, for which it was written.

E. W. HYDE.

SKEW ARCHES.

I propose in this paper to discuss to some extent three methods which have been employed in the construction of oblique or skew arches, and to make a comparison of their relative security, facility of construction, etc.

The three methods will be designated as,

1st. The Helicoidal method.

2d. The Logarithmic method.

3d. The " Corne de Vache " or Cow's-horn method.

The first two names are derived from the nature of the coursing and heading joint surfaces and their intersections with the soffit, and the third from the soffit itself, which is a warped surface that has been thus named. They will be considered in the order given above.

The following abbreviations will be used throughout the paper:

C j c, for coursing joint curve, or intersection of coursing joint with soffit.

H j c, for heading joint curve.

C j s, for coursing joint surface.

H j s, for heading joint surface.

H P, for the horizontal plane of projection.

V P, for the vertical plane of projection.

P F, for the plane of the face of the arch.

Ex. s, for the extradosal or outer surface of the arch.

THE HELICOIDAL METHOD.

In this method the C j s's and H j s's are both warped helicoids, and of course their intersections with the soffit helices.

Let C D D$_s$ C$_s$ be the projection of the soffit on the H P which coincides with the springing plane of the arch, and D′ V C$_s$ is a semicircle whose radius will be designated by r.

The Ex. s will be taken as a concentric cylinder projected in A B B$_2$ H$_2$ and B' V' A$_2$ and its radius will be designated by r.

To construct the C and H j c's we will first develop the soffit. Lay off O$_1$ T$=\pi$ $=3,1416\ r$; the points of the curve D E F C$_1$ may be found by the principles of descriptive geometry or by means of the equation of the curve, which we shall obtain. The latter method is much more accurate for construction upon a large scale.

Let $h = D'D_2$, and $\alpha =$ angle $C_2D_2D' =$ obliquity of the arch; $\therefore$ tang. $\alpha = \dfrac{2r}{h}$.

Also $\theta =$ variable angle sQD'. The origin will be taken first at O_1. We have from the figure

O$_1$ $\beta = x = r\ \theta$.

$O\ y = \frac{1}{2}\ h$, E $\beta = -\ y$.

$\therefore \dfrac{\frac{1}{2}h + y}{h} = \dfrac{r\ (1 - \cos\ \theta)}{2r} = \dfrac{1 - \cos\ \theta}{2}$

$\therefore \quad 1 - \cos\ \theta = \dfrac{h + 2y}{h}$

8

and $$\cos\theta = -\frac{2y}{h}$$

$$\therefore \quad \theta = \cos^{-1}\left(-\frac{2y}{h}\right)$$

whence $$x = r\cos^{-1}\left(-\frac{2y}{h}\right).$$

Solving for y we have

(1) $$y = -\frac{h}{2}\cos\frac{x}{r},$$

which is the equation of D E F C, with the origin at O_1. If the origin be moved to O_2 the equation becomes

(2) $$y = \frac{h}{2}\sin\frac{x}{r}.$$

From either of these equations the values of y for given values of x may be easily obtained by the aid of a table of natural sines and cosines.

Having constructed the curve D E F C_1, join D and C_1 by a straight line. This will be the development of a H j c. At O_2 draw O_2 S perpendicular to D C_1. O_2 S is the development of $\frac{1}{4}$ of a spire of the

helix which forms the C j c's, and corre-
sponds to the curve O P R.

The angle $TO_2S = TC_1O_2 = tang. -^1 \dfrac{\pi r}{}$

(3)
$$\therefore TS = O_2T \ tang \ TO_2S = \frac{\pi^2 r^2}{2\,h} = \tfrac{1}{4}\,\pi^2 r \ tan \ \alpha$$

Now divide D E F C_1 into a convenient
odd number of equal parts, so arranging
it as to cause one of the C j c's as δ D_2
to pass through D_r. The developments
of the C j c's are of course drawn parallel
to O_2 S through the points of division of
the curve D E F C_1. If it were not convenient to divide D E F C_1 in such a manner that a line through D_2 parallel to O_2S
would exactly pass through one of the
points of division, the direction of the
C j c's might be slightly changed, or the
divisions between D_2 δ and C_2 δ might be
made very slightly larger or smaller, as
the case required, then the divisions from
D to δ and from C_2 to δ'. The latter
method seems preferable, since it pre-
serves the perpendicularity between the
C and H j c's, and the difference in the

size of the voussoirs would be so small as
not to be noticeable.

All the courses below δ and δ_1 run out
into the abutment, and the impost must
be cut in steps, as shown in the figure,
into which the voussoirs will fit.

A G H B_1 is the development of the extrados, and the right line $x\,y$ that of a
helix in which one of the H j s's intersects the Ex. s. $O_4\,R_1$ is the development of the curve O L R_1, in which a
C j s intersects the Ex. s.

$$Tan\;x\;y\;O_s = \frac{h}{\pi r_1}.$$

$$Tan\;O_s\;O_4\;R = \frac{T\,\beta}{\tfrac{1}{2}\,\pi\,r_1} = \frac{\pi^2\,r^2}{2h} \div \frac{\pi\,r_1}{2} =$$

$$\frac{r}{r_1}, \frac{\pi\,r}{h} = \frac{\pi\,r}{2\,r_1}\;tan\;\alpha.$$

The C j s's are generated by a right
line moving on the axis O Q as one directrix, the helix O P R as a second, and
remaining always perpendicular to the
former. Hence the V P is a plane directer of the surface.

The details of the construction of a
skew arch by this method are fully developed in "A Practical and Theoretical
Essay on Oblique Bridges," by John
Watson Buck, M. Inst. C. E. He, however, makes the C and H j s's *hyperbolic
paraboloids* instead of helicoids, as follows: The corners of the voussoirs are
normals to the soffit at the intersection of
the H and C j c's, and hence are elements
of the warped helicoids, which *should*
form the H and C j s's. The points
where two of the normals on the same
side of the voussoir pierce the soffit are
joined by a right line, and this line is
moved on the normals as directrices in
such a manner as to pass over equal dis-
tances, measured on the normals in equal
times, by which operation a hyperbolic
paraboloid is generated. The accompanying figure is an exaggerated represen-
tation of the effect of cutting the stones
in this manner. A B C D and E F G H
are the developed introdosal surfaces of
two voussoirs in successive courses. If
the courses were not required to break

joints, the stones would fit perfectly, but as this is necessary to the stability of the arch, that portion of a stone which is too

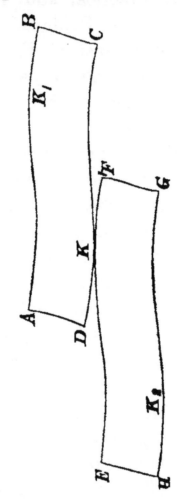

full will come opposite to the portion of the one in the next course which is likewise too full, and similarly the hollow portion of one opposite to the hollow portion of the next.

The truth of these statements will appear as follows: The hyperbolic paraboloid evidently cannot coincide with the helicoid, as they are surfaces con-structed according to a different law. The normals to the two adjacent corners of a voussoir are elements of both surfaces. The normal midway between these two is also an element common to the two surfaces. Hence it is evident from the mode of their genera-tion that the two surfaces intersect each other along each of these three lines. A section of the surfaces by a plane perpendicular to the middle nor-mal would give something like the accom-

panying figure, ⸺⸺ the straight line being the intersection with the hyper-bolic paraboloid and the curve that with the helicoid.

However, if the voussoirs are small compared with the whole arch, as in Fig. 1, the difference between the paraboloidal and helicoidal surfaces in the length of one voussoir will be exceedingly small, and the stones will fit with sufficient exactness for practical purposes. Nevertheless, the *tendency* is to cause the pressure to be unequally distributed, concentrating it at K, K₁, K₂ and at A, C, E and G. The difficulty of cutting the warped faces of the voussoirs is considerably diminished by this approximate method.

An investigation will now be made of the security of an arch constructed according to the helicoidal method.

In order that there may be *no* tendency in the successive courses to slide upon each other, it is evident that each C j s must be at every point normal to the direction of the pressure at that point. We shall consider first the direction of pressure as regards its parallelism to a certain vertical plane, without reference to the angle it may make at any point with the H P. This vertical plane is the place of the face of the arch. It is probable that the direction of pressure varies somewhat with reference to this plane in differ-

ent portions of the arch, especially if the
crown settles to any extent after removal
of the centre. Still it must be approximately parallel to the P F, otherwise the
portions near B and A, would be un-
supported and would consequently fall.
For the purposes of the investigation
then the direction of pressure will be
assumed to be in a plane parallel to the
P F, and from the results obtained we
shall be able to see without difficulty
the effect upon the security of the arch
which would be produced if the direction
of pressure were *not* parallel to the P F.
Proceeding then on this assumption, a
line drawn on the C j s of any voussoir
and lying in a plane perpendicular to the
P F and to the H P *ought* to be *horizontal*, but as this line would be the intersection of a warped helicoid by a plane not
containing an element of the surface, it
must be a *curve*, and can only be horizontal at a maximum or a minimum
point, at infinity, or at some singular point.
The intersection of the C j s of a voussoir
by a *horizontal* plane should give a line

perpendicular to the P F, but this line would be also a curve, and could have the required direction only at one or more points. It becomes necessary then to discover the nature of. these curves and the direction of their tangents at the point of piercing the soffit.

In Fig. 1 (Frontispiece) the curves Q P'₄ a, Q P'ₛ b, etc., are the vertical projections of the curves cut by the vertical planes, P₄ ℰ, Pₛ k, etc., from the helicoid whose directrices are the axis O Q and the helix O P R. The curve Q P'c has a maximum point at P P' where it pierces the soffit; all those above it have a maximum point *outside* the soffit, and those below it have one *inside* the same.

The curves O P₄ r, O Pₛ q, etc., are cut by horizontal planes through the points P₄ P'₄, Pₛ', etc. The curve through P is not drawn, but if it were it would be tangent at P to the line P h.

It is plain from inspection of these curves that the courses below P P' have a tendency to slide upon each other in a direction from A₂ towards A, which increases as the abutment is approached. In Fig. 1 this point P P' is on the tenth course from the abutment, and there are three coursing joints which would have a tendency to slide throughout their whole length with nothing to resist it except friction between the surfaces. The *partial* courses would be prevented from sliding by the steps cut in the impost. Above P P' the tendency to slide would be in the opposite direction, but would be so small as not to affect seriously the stability of the arch. This will be evident from inspection of the curves O P_1 p and O P_2 o.

We will now investigate these curves analytically and determine the position of the point P P'.

The distance T S, Fig. 1, is $\frac{1}{4}$ the height of one spire of the helix O P R, and from eq. (3) $T S = \dfrac{^2\pi r^2}{2 h} = \frac{1}{4} \pi^2 \ r \ tan \ \alpha.$

Call the height of one spire of the helix h_1, then

$$h_1 = \frac{2 \ \pi^2 \ r^2}{h} = \pi^2 \ r \ tan \ \alpha.$$

Let O be the origin of coörds, the axis of the cylinder, O Q, the axis of z, O T the axis of x, and the axis of y a vertical line through O. Then we shall have for the helix O P R,

$$\frac{\theta - \dfrac{\pi}{2}}{2\,\pi} = \frac{z}{h_1} \; ;$$

whence $\theta = \dfrac{2\,\pi\,z}{h_1} + \dfrac{\pi}{2}.$

Also

$$x = r\,cos\,\theta = r\,cos\left(\frac{2\,\pi\,z}{h_1} + \frac{\pi}{2}\right) = -r\,sin\frac{2\,\pi\,z}{h_1},$$

or substituting for h, its value

$$(4) \qquad x = -\,r\,sin\,\frac{h\,z}{\pi\,r^2}$$

which is the equation of O P R, the projection on X Z of one of the C j c's. The vertical projection, or the projection on X Y of this helix is

$$(5) \qquad x^2 + y^2 = r^2.$$

To obtain the equation of the C j s, we

must find the equations of an element, and then eliminate the constant which fixes its position. Let one equation of the element be

(6) $\qquad z = z_1.$

To find the equation in terms of x and y, substitute in the equation

$$\frac{y - y_1}{x - x_1} = \frac{y_1 - y_2}{x_1 - x_2}$$

of a line through two points the proper values of x_1, x_2, y_1 and y_2. We have since all the elements cut the axis of z,

$$x_1 = o \text{ and } y_1 = o.$$

Substituting from (6) in (4)

$$x_2 = - r \sin\frac{h z_1}{\pi r^2},$$

and substituting this value of x_2 in (5),

$$y_2 = \sqrt{r^2 - r^2 \sin^2\frac{h z_1}{\pi r^2}} = r\sqrt{1 - \sin^2\frac{h z_1}{\pi r^2}}$$

$$= r \cos\frac{h z_1}{\pi r^2}.$$

$$\therefore \frac{y}{x} = - \frac{r \cos \dfrac{h\,z_1}{\pi\,r^3}}{r \sin \dfrac{h\,z_1}{\pi\,r^3}} = - \cot \frac{h\,z_1}{\pi\,r^3};$$

or making z_1 general by dropping the subscript,

$$(7) \qquad y = - x \cot \frac{h\,z}{\pi\,r^3},$$

which is the equation of a C j s.

Now, intersect this surface by a vertical plane perpendicular to the P F, whose equation is

$$(8) \qquad z = \frac{2\,r}{h} (a_1 - x),$$

in which a_1 is the intercept on X.

$$(9) \quad \therefore\ y = - x \cot \left(\frac{2\,(a_1 - x)}{\pi\,r} \right)$$

which is the equation of the curves Q P′ c, etc.

In equation (9) if

$$x = 0, \qquad y = 0;$$

$$\text{if } x = a_1 - \frac{(2\,n - 1)\,\pi^2\,r}{4},$$

$$y = -x \cot \frac{(2n-1)\pi}{2} = 0,$$

n being an integer;

if $x = a_1 - \dfrac{n\pi^2 r}{2},$

$$y = -x \cot n\pi = \curvearrowleft,$$

n as before being an integer. Hence the curve has an infinite number of branches. It is to be noticed that equation (9) *does not contain h*, the only constants being π, a_1 and r, *hence the form of the curves $Q P' c$, $Q P_1' d$, etc., is entirely independent of the obliquity of the arch.* We will next differentiate equation (9) for a maximum.

$$\frac{dy}{dx} = -\cot\left(\frac{2(a_1-x)}{\pi r}\right) - \frac{2x}{\pi r \sin^2\left(\frac{2(a_1-x)}{\pi r}\right)}$$

Let $\dfrac{2(a_1-x)}{\pi r} = u$

(10) $\quad \therefore \quad \dfrac{dy}{dx} = -\cot u - \dfrac{2x}{\pi r \sin^2 u}$

For a maximum

$$\cot u = -\frac{2x}{\pi r \sin^2 u}.$$

$$(11) \therefore x_{ymax} = - \frac{\pi \, r \, sin \, u \, cos \, u}{2}$$

By solving equation (11) the values of x for which y is a maximum or minimum can be obtained. It is only capable, however, of an approximate solution, but if we obtain the x co-ordinate of the intersection of the locus of equation (9) with the circle

$$(12) \qquad x^2 + y^2 = r_2^2,$$

in which r_2 may have any value, and place this value of x equal to that in equation (11), we shall obtain the value of x_{ymax} when the maximum point is at the intersection of the two curves.

$\therefore$ substituting from (9) in (12)

$$x_i^2 + x_i^2 \, cot^2 \, u_i = r_2^2$$

$$x_i^2 \, (1 + cot^2 \, u_i) = x_i^2 \, cosec^2 \, u_i = r_2^2.$$

$$(13) \qquad \therefore \quad x_i = r_2 \, sin \, u_i.$$

$\therefore$ by (11) and (13),

$$r_2 \, sin \, u_i = - \frac{\pi \, r \, sin \, u_i \, cos \, u_i}{2}$$

$$\therefore \quad cos \, u_i = - \frac{2 \, r_2}{\pi \, r}$$

$$\frac{2\,(a_1 - x_1)}{\pi\,r} = u_1 = \cos^{-1}\left(-\frac{2\,r_2}{\pi\,r}\right)$$

$$\therefore\ x_1 = a_1 \doteq \frac{\pi\,r}{2}\cos^{-1}\left(\frac{2\,r_2}{\pi\,r}\right).$$

Denoting by x_{m1} the value of x for which y is a maximum when the locus of (9) is subject to the condition of having a maximum point at its intersection with $x^2 + y^2 = r_2^2$, and substituting the value of x just found in the 2d member of (13), we have

$$x_{m1} = r_2\,\sin\left\{\frac{\left(2\,a_1 - a_1 + \frac{\pi\,r}{2}\cos^{-1}\left(-\frac{2r_2}{\pi r}\right)\right)}{\pi\,r}\right\}$$

$$= r_2\,\sin\cos^{-1}\left(\frac{2\,r_2}{\pi\,r}\right)$$

$$= r_2\,\sin\sin^{-1}\sqrt{1 - \frac{4\,r_2^2}{\pi^2\,r^2}}$$

$$= r_2\,\sqrt{\frac{\pi^2\,r^2 - 4\,r_2^2}{\pi^2\,r^2}}$$

$$(14)\ \therefore\ x_{m1} = r_2\,\frac{\sqrt{\pi^2\,r^2 - 4\,r_2^2}}{\pi\,r}$$

Let $r_2 = r$, this being the condition that the maximum point shall be at the point where the locus of (9) pierces the soffit, and we have

$$(15) \quad x_{ml} = \frac{r}{\pi}\sqrt{\pi^2 - 4} = r\ cos\ \tau.$$

Whence

$$(16) \quad x_{ml} = 0.77118r = r\ cos\ 39°\ 32'\ 23''.$$

This value of τ may also be found by means of the curves OP_1p, OP_2o, etc. Intersect the surface of equation (7) by the horizontal plane

$$(17) \qquad\qquad y = b.$$

$$\therefore\quad b = -x\ cot\ \frac{h\ z}{\pi\ r^2}$$

$$(18) \quad \text{or} \quad x = -b\ tan\ \frac{h\ z}{\pi\ r^2},$$

the equation of the curves $OP_1 p$, etc.

Differentiating

$$(19) \quad \frac{dz}{dx} = -\frac{\pi\ r^2}{b\ h}\ cos^2\frac{h\ z}{\pi\ r^2}$$

If $z = \pm\dfrac{\pi^2\ r^2}{2\ h}$ in (18) and (19) we have

$$x = \backsim \text{ and } \frac{dz}{dx} = 0,$$

showing that the lines $z = \pm \dfrac{\pi^2 r^2}{2 h}$ are

asymptotes of the curves.

Intersect the circle $x^2 + y^2 = r_2^2$ by $y = b$

$$\therefore \quad x_i = \pm \sqrt{r_2^2 - b^2}.$$

Substitute this value of x in (18) and

$$\pm_1 \sqrt{{}_1 r_2^2 - b^2} = - b \tan \frac{h z_i}{\pi r^2}; \text{ whence}$$

$$(20) \quad z_1 = \frac{\pi r^2}{h} \tan^{-1} \left(\frac{\mp \sqrt{r_2^2 - b^2}}{b} \right)$$

z_i is the z co-ordinate of the point in which the locus of (18) pierces the cylinder, concentric with the soffit, whose radius is r_2.

Substitute from (20) in (19), thus

$$\frac{dz_i}{dx_i} = - \frac{\pi r^2}{b h} \cos^2 \left\{ \tan^{-1} \left(\frac{\pm \sqrt{r_2^2 - b^2}}{b} \right) \right\}$$

$$= - \frac{\pi r^2}{b h} \left\{ \cos \cos^{-1} \frac{1}{\sqrt{1 + \frac{r_2^2 - b^2}{b^2}}} \right\}^2$$

$$(21) \qquad = -\frac{\pi\, b}{h}\left(\frac{r}{r_2}\right)^2$$

If $r_2 = r$, when the cylinder mentioned above becomes the soffit,

$$(22) \qquad \frac{dz_t}{dx_t} = -\frac{\pi\, b}{h},$$

which is the tangent of the angle between the tangent to the locus of (18) and the axis of x at the point where the locus pierces the soffit. If we make the condition that

$$(23) \qquad \frac{dz_t}{dx_t} = -\frac{2\, r}{h};$$

that is, that the tangent at this point shall be perpendicular to the P F, we have from (22) and (23)

$$\frac{\pi\, b_1}{h} = \frac{2\, r}{h}$$

$$(24) \therefore b_1 = \frac{2\, r}{\pi} = 0.63662\, r = r\, sin\, 39°\, 32'\, 23'''$$

which agrees with equation (16).

It is thus apparent that in an arch constructed by this method the portions below PP' or beyond the line $\eta\gamma$ on the development, should be *omitted;* *i.e.,* the arch should be *always segmental* with a span not exceeding

$2\ r\ \cos\ \tau = 2\ r\ \cos\ 39°\ 32'\ 23'' = 1.54236r,$

provided that there is to be no tendency in the successive courses to slide on one another. The amount of this tendency to slide and its relation to the obliquity of the arch will next be investigated.

Let us obtain an expression for the angle $\angle P_4\ \mu$ between the tangent line to $O\ P_4\ r$ at P_4 and the line $P_4\ \angle$ perpendicular to the P F. Let $\angle P_4\ \mu = \theta'$ then, equation (22),

$$\theta' = tan^{-1}\frac{2\ r}{h} - tan^{-1}\frac{\pi\ b}{h}$$

(25)
$$\therefore tan\ \theta' = \left(tan^{-1}\frac{2\ r}{h} - tan^{-1}\frac{\pi b}{h}\right) =$$

$$\frac{\dfrac{2\ r}{h} - \dfrac{\pi\ b}{h}}{1 + \dfrac{2\ \pi\ b\ r}{h^2}} = \frac{h\ (2\ r - \pi\ b)}{h^2 + 2\ \pi\ b\ r}$$

If $h = o,\ tan\ \theta' = o,\ \therefore\ \theta' = o.$
If $h = \infty\ tan\ \theta' = o,\ \therefore\ \theta' = o.$

θ' must be equal to θ when $tan\ \theta' = o$ because it can never equal, much less exceed 90°; for if it *can* equal 90°, then we must have from (25)

$$h^2 + 2\ \pi\ b\ r = 0\ ;$$
$$\therefore\ h = \sqrt{-\ 2\ \pi\ b\ r}\ ;$$

i. e., h must be imaginary. It follows that there must be some value of h for which $tan\ \theta'$ and therefore θ', is a maximum. By placing the first differential co-efficient of the function with reference to $h = s$, we find this value to be

$$(26) \qquad h = \sqrt{2\ \pi\ b\ r}.$$

By this equation $h = 2\,r\ cot\ \alpha = 1.0445\,r,$

when $b = r\ sin\ 10°\ \therefore\ \underset{\theta'\ \text{max}}{\alpha} = 62°\ 25'$ for

this value of b.

Now the tendency to slide at any point, as $P_4\ P_4'$, depends upon the angle between the normal to the C j s at that point and the direction of the pressure. This last we have assumed to be in a plane parallel to the P F. We will now

assume for the purposes of the investigation that it coincides at the point P_4P_4'
with the direction of the tangent at that
point to the ellipse cut from the soffit by
a plane through the point parallel to the
P F. Let $p_1 =$ tangent of angle between
ground line and tangent line to curve
$Q P_4'$ a at the point P_4'; then the tangent
of the angle between the tan line to this
curve in space at the point $P_4 P_4'$ and
the H P will be $= p_1 \cos \alpha$.

Let $p_2 =$ tangent of angle between a
vertical line and the tangent line to the
circle $D' V C_2$ at the point $P_4' =$ angle
$P_4' Q C_2$, then the tangent of the angle
between a vertical and the tangent
line at $P_4 P_4'$ to the section of the soffit
parallel to the P F will be $= p_2$
cosec α.

Now to find the angle between the
normal at $P_4 P_4'$ to the C j s, and the tangent to the section parallel to the P F,
we have given two sides and the included angle of a spherical triangle, the included angle being θ'.

Let N $=$ angle between normal to

j s, at P_4 P_4' and vertical = angle be-

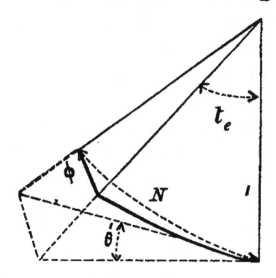

tween tangent plane to C j s at P_4 P_4' an
H P, then we find the value of tan N to
be tan $N = p_1 \cos \alpha \operatorname{cosec} \theta'$.

$$(27) \quad \therefore \sin N = \frac{p_1 \cos \alpha \operatorname{cosec} \theta'}{\sqrt{1 + p_1^2 \cos^2 \alpha \operatorname{cosec}_2 \theta'}}$$

$$(28) \quad \cos N = \frac{1}{\sqrt{1 + p_1^2 \cos^2 \alpha \operatorname{cosec}^2 \theta^1}}$$

and if $t_e = tan^{-1}(p_2 \operatorname{cosec} \alpha)$, we have

$$(29) \quad \sin t_e = \frac{p_2 \operatorname{cosec} \alpha}{\sqrt{1 + p_2^2 \operatorname{cosec}^2 \alpha}}$$

$$(30) \quad \cos t_e = \frac{1}{\sqrt{1 + p_2^2 \operatorname{consec}^2 \alpha}}.$$

By spherical trigonometry

(31) $\cos \Phi = \cos N \cos t_e + \sin N \sin t_e \cos \theta'$; whence, by substitution

(32)
$$\cos \Phi = \frac{1 + p_1 p^2 \cot \alpha \cot \theta'}{\sqrt{(1 + p_1^2 \cos^2 \alpha \ cosec^2 \ \theta')\ (1 + p_2^2 \ cosec^2 \ \alpha)}}$$

Multiplying numerator and denominator by $\sin \alpha \sin \theta'$, this becomes

(33)
$$\cos \Phi = \frac{\sin \alpha \sin \theta' + p_1 p_2 \cos \alpha \cos \theta'}{\sqrt{(\sin^2 \theta' + p_1^2 \cos^2 \alpha)\ (p_2^2 + \sin^2 \alpha)}}$$

If in this equation $\alpha = o$, then by equation (25), since $h = 2\,r \cot \alpha$, $\theta' = o$, and

hence $\cos \Phi = \dfrac{p_1 p_2}{p_1 p_2} = 1$, $\therefore \Phi = o$.

If $\alpha = 90°$—i.e., the obliquity$=0$—by (25) $\theta' = 0$, and hence $\cos \Phi = \frac{0}{0}$ indeterminate. The reason for this is, that the tangent lines to the curves $\natural\ P_4 "$ $QP_4' a$, and $OP_4 r "P'_4 \pi$ by which we have fixed the position of the tangent plane *coincide* when $\alpha = 90°$. The value towards which cos Φ *approaches*, however, is unity, as α approaches 90°, for from the relations between the quantities it is evident that when $\theta' = 0$, N must equal t_0, and hence by equation (31),

cos $\Phi = cos^2 t_0 + sin^2 t_0 = 1$; ∴ $\Phi = o$.

It follows, therefore, that there must be some value of α for which cos Φ is a minimum, and therefore Φ a maximum, for any given values of p_1 and p_2. Owing to the complexity of the expression for cos Φ, this value would be very difficult to obtain by differentiation; but it can be determined approximately by calculating a series of values of cos Φ for different values of α. This has been done, with the following results:

The point for which the calculations are made is P_4 P'_4, for which

$$x = -r \cos 10°, \ y = b = r \sin 10°, \ z =$$

$$\frac{4 \pi^2 r^2}{9 h} p_2 = tan \ 10°, \text{ and } p_1 = 0.47011 =$$

tan 25° 10′ 43″, the value of p_1 being found by equation (10).

TABLE I.

When $\alpha = 60°$, $\theta' = 34° 42' 41''$, and $\Phi = 14° 57' 30''$

" $\alpha = 40°$, $\theta' = 27° 10' 00''$, " $\Phi = 25° 27' 00''$

" $\alpha = 30°$, $\theta' = 21° 3' 00''$, " $\Phi = 31° 00' 00''$

" $\alpha = 20°$, $\theta' = 14° 19' 50''$, " $\Phi = 34° 44' 00''$

" $\alpha = 10°$, $\theta' = 7° 14' 50''$, ' $\Phi = 29° 57' 00''$

From this table it appears that Φ is a maximum when α has some value not far from 20°.

If the point considered be P P' for which $x = r \cos \tau = r \cos 39° 32' 23,''$ and
$$y = b = r \sin 39° 32' 23'',$$

we have $\theta' = o$ and $p, = o_1$ ∴ in equation (33) $cos\ \Phi = \frac{o}{o}$, and from the same considerations as when $\alpha = 90°$, we find

$$cos\ \Phi = 1, \text{ whence } \Phi = o,$$

without reference to what the value of α may be.

If, as is very probably the case, the direction of pressure is *not* exactly parallel to the P F, but inclines somewhat towards the plane of the right section of the soffit, the effect will be to *increase* the tendency to slide on the C j s's. Near the springing plane, however, the direction of pressure in a vertical plane will not be exactly parallel to the tangent to the oblique section, but will make a *less* angle with the H P, which will tend, especially when the obliquity is considerable, to counteract the previously mentioned effect. This refers to portions of the arch *below* P P′ for which $y = r\ sin\ 39°\ 32'\ 23''$; *above* this, the tendency to sliding being in the *opposite direction ;* if the line of pressure incline towards the plane of right section, it will decrease this tendency, and thus add to the stability of the arch. It is evident from inspection of the table of values of Φ that a *full centred* arch should not be built by this method unless with a small obliquity, and then it would need to be thoroughly supported by the spandrels.

These results differ entirely from those obtained in Chap. VII. of Buck's treatise on oblique arches already referred to ; in fact, are in direct opposition to them. He derives a formula for the value of τ *dependent upon the obliquity of the arch*, so that τ decreases with α, or as the obliquity increases, and infers therefrom that the safety of the arch *increases* as it becomes more oblique up to about $25°$. I should state that his τ has a slightly different signification from mine. He undertakes to find the point at which the curves Q P′c, Q P′d, etc., cut the intrados and extrados at the *same height* above the H P, and calls the angle included between a radius drawn to this point of the intrados and the H P the angle τ. It will be

evident from inspection of the drawing
that this would give to τ a somewhat
greater value than I have obtained, but
still *independent* of α, since the only constants in equation (9) are a_1 π, and r.

The following table taken from his
book gives the values of τ obtained by
Buck from his formula for certain values
of α, from which he derives his inferences
with reference to the security of oblique
arches.

TABLE FROM BUCK'S ESSAY ON OBLIQUE BRIDGES.

When $\alpha = 65°$, then $\tau = 27° 17'$
" $\alpha = 55°$, " $\tau = 25° 13'$
" $\alpha = 45°$, " $\tau = 21° 47'$
" $\alpha = 35°$, " $\tau = 15° 38'$
" $\alpha = 25°40'$ " $\tau = 0° 0'$

Immediately under this table he remarks, "It will be observed that the last
angle is given 25° 40', at which the point
τ descends to the level of the axis of the
cylinder, and *the whole semicircle is safe*."*
By looking at the table of values of Φ it

---

* The *italics* are mine.

will be seen that, for this value of α, Φ will be about 32° or 33° at 10° above the springing plane, τ of course being 39° 32′ 23″ instead of o, and hence the arch will be anything but safe if a complete semi-cylinder.

One incorrect assumption made by Buck in his derivation of the formula for the value of τ is as follows. He says: " It may be shown that the tangent of the angle which the tangent to the intradosal spiral makes with the horizon diminishes as cos τ." He does not show it, however.

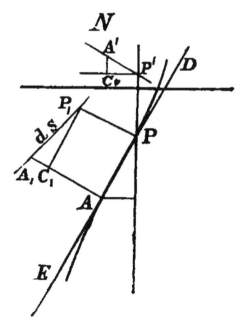

Call the above mentioned angle ψ, and
the angle between the tangent to the
helix at any point and axis of the cylinder
β, then the true relation is

$$sin\ \psi = sin\ \beta\ cos\ \tau$$

$$tan\ \psi = \frac{sin\ \beta\ cos\ \tau}{\sqrt{1 - sin^2\ \beta\ cos^2\ \tau.}}$$

In the figure suppose A P to be the
horizontal projection of an element $d\,s$ of
the helix coinciding with the tangent line
D E. A′ P′ is its vertical projection, and
$A_1\ P_1$ its revolved position about a horizontal line in a vertical plane through P.
The angle $A_1\ P_1\ C_1 = \psi$, and the angle
C A′ P′ $= \tau$.

∴ $ds\ sin\ \psi = A_1\ C_1 = A'\ C = A'\ P'\ cos\ \tau$;
but A′ P′ $= ds\ sin\ \beta$;

∴ $sin\ \psi = sin\ \beta\ cos\ \tau.$

At the springing plane the tangent to
the elliptical section parallel to the P F
becomes vertical, and the value of Φ is

$$(34)\ \ tan\ \Phi = \frac{h}{\pi\ r} = \frac{2}{\pi}\ cot\ \alpha.$$

At the crown it is

(35) $\quad tan\ \Phi = tan\ \theta' = \dfrac{(2-\pi)\ cot\ \alpha}{2\ cot^2\ \alpha + \pi}$

The following is a table similar to table I, giving the values of Φ at the crown and springing plane, derived from equations (34) and (35).

TABLE II.

	At the Crown.	At the Springing Plane.
When $\alpha=60°$	$-\Phi_c,= 9°\ 50'$	$\Phi_{sp}=18°\ 20'$
" $\alpha=50°$	$-\Phi_c,=11°\ 53'$	$\Phi_{sp}=28°\ 7'$
" $\alpha=40°$	$-\Phi_c,=12°\ 49'$	$\Phi_{sp}=37°\ 11'$
" $\alpha=30°$	$-\Phi_c,= 9°\ 16'$	$\Phi_{sp}=47°\ 48'$

$\Phi_c = \theta_c'$ is a maximum by equation (26) when $\alpha = 38°\ 35'$, for which value of α we find $\theta_c = 12°\ 50'$.

At the angle $\alpha = 25°\ 40'$—the last one given in the table extracted from Buck's work—the line which he finds to be horizontal makes an angle with the H P of a little more than $29°\ 51'$, that being the angle between the tangent to the locus of equation (9) at the point R» C_2 and the H P.

It will be noticed that the negative sign of Φ_0 in Table II. comes from the fact that in equation (35) π is greater than 2. It indicates that the tendency to sliding is in the *opposite direction* from what it is below τ.

LOGARITHMIC METHOD.

In this method the soffit is cylindrical, as in the last, and the case considered will be that in which the right section is circular.

The heading joints are *planes* parallel to the P F, which, therefore, cut the soffit in ellipses, which are the h j c's. The c j c's are drawn on the soffit in such a manner as to cut each h j c at *right angles*.

Now, the angle between any two lines of the soffit remains unchanged after the development ; hence, the developed c j c's must cut the developed h j c's at right angles. Also, if two lines be perpendicular to each other, their projections on a plane parallel to one of them will be perpendicular; hence, if the arch be projected upon a plane parallel to the P F, the vertical projections of the c j c's will cut the ellipses which are the vertical projections of the h j c's at right angles. These principles will be used in obtaining the equations of the curves.

Let A B B, A, » B' V' A, be the projections of the Ex. S., and C D D, C, » D' V C, those of the soffit. O Q is the axis of the cylinder, D C₁ C₂ D₂ is the development of the soffit to be constructed from the projections, or by means of ordinates found from equations (1) or (2).

The developed h j c's are all parallel to D E O, F C₁, and hence may be drawn from a pattern constructed by means of this curve. Divide D D₂ into such a number of equal parts as will make the voussoirs of convenient size, and draw the h j c's through the points of division by the pattern. The length of one of these curves is equal to that of a semi-ellipse cut from the soffit by a P F, and is calculated by the aid of the following formula, obtained by integrating the differential of the elliptical arc.

If S = length of semi ellipse, a = semi-major axis and e = eccentricity, then

$$(36) \quad S = \pi a\left(1 - \frac{e^2}{4} - \frac{3\,e^4}{64} - \frac{5\,e^6}{768} - \text{etc.}\right)$$

The *middle* h j c, *n o*, must be next divided up into a convenient odd num-ber of equal parts. The division is done on the middle line, in order that the two faces of the arch may be alike. We will next find the equation of the curve k O₂ *m* of which the c j c's on the develop-ment of the soffit are portions.

We have already found the equation of D E F C₁, equation (1), in considering the helicoidal method. With the origin at O₁, it is

$$y = -\frac{h}{2}\cos\frac{x}{r}$$

Differentiating

$$(37) \qquad \frac{dy}{dx} = \frac{h}{2\,r}\sin\frac{x}{r}$$

If k O₂ *m* cut D E O₂ F C₁ at right angles,

we must have, at the point of intersection,

$$1 + \frac{dy}{dx} \cdot \frac{dy'}{dx'} = o, \text{ or } \frac{dy'}{dx'} = - \frac{dx}{dy}$$

in which $\frac{dy'}{dx'}$ is the differential co-effi-cient of the curve to be found. Substitute the value of $\frac{dx}{dy}$ from equation (37).

$$\therefore \frac{dy'}{dx'} = - \frac{2r}{h \sin \frac{x}{r}}, \text{ or dropping the}$$

primes, since the x and y in both mem-bers of the equation refer to the same point,

$$dy = - \frac{2r}{h} \cdot \frac{dx}{\sin \frac{x}{r}}.$$

$\therefore$ Integrating

$$(38) \quad y = - \frac{2r^2}{h} l_e \tan \frac{x}{2r} + c,$$

in which l_e signifies Naperian logarithm.

If we let $y = o$, when $x = \frac{\pi r}{2}$, this being

the condition that the curve shall pass through O_2, we have

$$o = -\frac{2\,r^3}{h}\,l_e\,(1) + c;$$

$\therefore\ c = o,$ and

$$(39)\quad y = -\frac{2\,r^3}{h}\,l_e\,\tan\frac{x}{2\,r}.$$

If we move the origin to O_2 by placing $x = x' + \dfrac{\pi\,r}{2}$, equation (39) becomes

$$y' = -\frac{2\,r^3}{h}\,l_e\,\tan\left(\frac{x' + \dfrac{\pi\,r}{2}}{2\,r}\right) =$$

$$-\frac{2\,r^3}{h}\,l_e\,\tan\left(\frac{x'}{2\,r}+\frac{\pi}{4}\right);$$

or dropping primes and reducing

$$(40)\quad y = -\frac{2\,r^3}{h}\,l_e\left(\frac{1 + \tan\dfrac{x}{2\,r}}{1 - \tan\dfrac{x}{2\,r}}\right)$$

In (40) if

$$x = o, y = -\frac{2\,r^2}{h}\,l_\bullet\,(1) = o;$$

$$x = \frac{\pi\,r}{2}, y = -\frac{2\,r^2}{h}\,l_\bullet\,(\infty) = -\infty;$$

$$x = -\frac{\pi\,r}{2}, y = -\frac{2\,r^2}{h}\,l_\bullet\,(o) = +\infty.$$

∴ the curve is asymptotic to the right lines

$$x = \pm\frac{\pi\,r}{2}; \quad i.\,e.,\text{ to } l \text{ X and D D}'.$$

If the obliquity of the arch in fig. (2) were in the *opposite direction*, the right hand members of equations (1), (38), (39), and (40) would all be *positive*.

To adapt equation (39) to convenient computation, let $x = n\,\pi\,r$, which is equivalent to dividing the distance $\pi\,r =$ O_1 X into n equal parts, for which ordinates are to be calculated.

∴ Substituting common logarithms for Naperian,

$$(41)\; y = -\frac{2\,r^2}{h}\cdot\frac{1}{\text{M}}l_\bullet\,tan\,\frac{n\,\pi}{2},$$

in which $l_{\bullet}$ signifies common logarithm, and **M** is the modulus of the common system. From this equation any number of ordinates may be easily calculated for the construction of the curve $k\,O_2\,m$.

The equation of the curve **K O P P$_2$** will next be found. This is the horizontal projection of the curve on the soffit of which $k\,O_2\,m$ is the development. Its vertical projection is of course the semicircle D′ V C$_2$. It is plain that for any value of y the x for the new equation will bear a certain relation to the x of equation (39), and hence may be derived from it. Call the co-ordinates of **K O P** x' and y', x and y being those of equation (39),

$$\therefore\ x' = -\,r\left(1-\cos\frac{x}{r}\right);\ \text{whence}\ x =$$

$$r\,\cos^{-1}\!\left(\frac{x'+r}{r}\right),\ \text{and}\ y' = y,\ \text{the origin}$$

being at O$_1$.

Substituting in equation (39) and omitting primes,

$$(42)\quad y = -\,\frac{2\,r^2}{h}\,l_{\bullet}\,\tan\tfrac{1}{2}\left[\cos^{-1}\!\left(\frac{x+r}{r}\right)\right]^{\!\frac{1}{2}}$$

In (42) change the origin to O, and we have

$$(43) \quad y = -\frac{2\,r^2}{h}\, l_\bullet \tan \tfrac{1}{2}\left(\cos^{-1}\frac{x}{r}\right).$$

Now we have by trigonometry

$$\cos^{-1}\frac{x}{r} = \tan^{-1}\frac{\sqrt{1-\frac{x^2}{r^2}}}{\frac{x}{r}} = \tan^{-1}\frac{\sqrt{r^2-x^2}}{x}$$

also

$$\tan \tfrac{1}{2}\left(\left(\tan^{-1}\frac{\sqrt{r^2-x^2}}{x}\right)\right) = \frac{-1+\sqrt{1+\frac{r^2-x^2}{x^2}}}{\frac{\sqrt{r^2-x^2}}{x}}$$

$$= \frac{r-x}{\sqrt{r^2-x^2}} = \sqrt{\frac{r-x}{r+x}}$$

Substituting in (43) we have

$$(44)\; y = \frac{-2r^2}{h}l_\bullet\sqrt{\frac{r-x}{r+x}} = \frac{r^2}{h}l_\bullet\left(\frac{r+x}{r-x}\right),$$

which is the equation of K O P with the origin at O, O Q being the axis of y.

In (44) if $x = 0$, $y = \dfrac{r^2}{h} \, l_\bullet (1) = 0$

" $x = r$, $y = \dfrac{r^2}{h} \, l_\bullet (\infty) = \infty$

" $x = -r$, $y = \dfrac{r^2}{h} \, l_\bullet(0) = -\infty.$

Equation (39) solved for x is:

(45) $x = 2 \, r \, tan^{-1} \, e^{-\frac{h\,y}{2\,r^2}}$

in which e is the base of the Naperian system of logarithms. It is sometimes desirable to consider y as the independent variable, in which oase the equation takes this form.

We will now give a table of values ot

$\dfrac{1}{M} l_\bullet \, tan \, \dfrac{n \, \pi}{2}$ corresponding to a series

of values of n, also the values of x in equation (44) for which the ordinates are equal to the corresponding ordinates of the ourve $k \, O_2 \, m$.

TABLE III.

Values of n in equation (41.)	Values of $\frac{1}{M} l_a \tan \frac{n \pi}{2}$.	Values of x in Equation (44) for which y is equal to the y of Equation (41).	REMARKS.
0.01	— 4.2331	0.99951r	N.B.—The values of x in column 3 are to be laid off from the *axis* of the *cylinder* as the axis of y. *In equation* (41) *the axis of y is* $O_1 D_2$. To obtain the corresponding values of x for the curve I O L M, *substitute* r_1 *for r in the* 3d column, the axis of y being the same.
0.02	— 3.4601	0.99803r	
0.03	— 3.0541	0.99556r	
0,04	— 2.7659	0.99211r	
0.05	— 2.5421	0.98769r	
0.10	— 1.8427	0.95106r	
0.15	— 1.4266	0.89101r	
0.20	— 1.1240	0.80902r	
0.25	— 0.8810	0.70711r	
0.30	— 0.6742	0.58779r	
0.35	— 0.4897	0.45399r	
0.40	— 0.3195	0.30902r	
0.45	— 0.1577	0.15643r	
0.50	— 0.0000	0.00000r	

By means of this table the curves k O_1 m and K O P may be easily and accurately constructed, as well as the curves I O L M and N R O$_4$ for the Ex s.

For the curve I O L M, which is the

intersection of a c j s, with a cylinder concentric with the soffit, we have if x be the abscissa of K O P, x' the abscissa of I O L M and r_1 the radius of the concentric cylinder,

$$\frac{x}{x'} = \frac{r}{r_1}, \text{ or } x = \frac{rx'}{r_1}.$$

This value in equation (44) gives

$$(46) \quad y = \frac{r^2}{h} \, l_e\left(\frac{r_1+x}{r_1-x}\right) \text{(primes omitted)}.$$

For the curve N R O$_4$ which is the development of I O L M, calling the abscissa of k O$_2$ m x, and that of N R O$_4$ x', we have

$$\frac{x}{x'} = \frac{r}{r_1}; \therefore x = \frac{rx'}{r_1},$$

which, in equation (40), gives, omitting primes,

$$(47) \quad y = -\frac{2\,r^2}{h} \, l_e\left(\frac{1 + tan\,\dfrac{x}{2\,r_1}}{1 - tan\,\dfrac{x}{2\,r_1}}\right)$$

which is the equation of N R O$_4$ with the origin at O$_4$. The ordinates for this

curve are the same as those for the curve
k O, m when we give the proper values
to x, that is, make $x = n \pi r_1$, and measure it from the line B_1 B_2 as the axis of
ordinates.

The curve S V' T is a projection of the
curve K O P P_1 on a plane parallel to the
P F, of which p q is the horizontal trace.
In constructing an arch by this method
it would be desirable to project it on
such a plane, and hence this curve would
be needed. It cuts at right angles the
projection on its plane of any ellipse cut
from the soffit by a plane parallel to the
P F, and its equation is found by a pro-
cess similar to that by which equation
(39) was obtained. Let g p be the axis
of x and O' V' the axis of y. The equation of the ellipses to which the curve is
to be normal at point of cutting is

(48) $b^2 (x - a_1)^2 + a^2 y^2 = a^2 b^2$

in which a_1 is the variable abscissa of the
centre. Differentiating

$$\frac{dy}{dx} = - \frac{b^2 (x - a_1)}{a^2 y}$$ or substituting value
of a_1 from (48)

$$\frac{dy}{dx} = \frac{b\sqrt{b^2 - y^2}}{ay}$$

This in the formula $1 + \frac{dy}{dx} \cdot \frac{dy'}{dx'} = 0$,

gives $\frac{dy'}{dx'} = -\frac{ay}{b\sqrt{b^2 - y^2}}$; or, dropping

primes, since x and y in the two members refer to the same point,

$$dx = -\frac{b}{a} y^{-1} dy \sqrt{b^2 - y^2}.$$

Whence, by integration

$$x = \frac{b}{a} \left\{ b\, l. \sqrt{\frac{b + \sqrt{b^2 - y^2}}{b - \sqrt{b^2 - y^2}}} - \sqrt{b^2 - y^2} \right\} + c$$

If we let $x = o$ where $y = b$—i. e., place the centre of the curve at O'—then $c = o$, and

(49)

$$x = \frac{b}{a} \left\{ b\, l. \sqrt{\frac{b + \sqrt{b^2 - y^2}}{b - \sqrt{b^2 - y^2}}} - \sqrt{b^2 - y^2} \right\}$$

This curve is symmetrical about both axes of reference, and is asymptotic to the axis of x.

To obtain (49) in a convenient form for computation, place $y = n\,b$, then

$$(50)\ x = \frac{b^2}{a}\left\{ l_e \sqrt{\frac{1+\sqrt{1-n^2}}{1-\sqrt{1-n^2}}} - \sqrt{1-n^2} \right\}$$

From this equation have been calculated the values of the parenthesis for a series of values of n, as given in the following table.

TABLE IV.

Values of n.	Values of $\dfrac{a\,x}{b^2}$.
0.1	$\pm$ 2.000
0.2	$\pm$ 1.313
0.3	$\pm$ 0.921
0.4	$\pm$ 0.650
0.5	$\pm$ 0.450
0.6	$\pm$ 0.299
0.7	$\pm$ 0.184
0.8	$\pm$ 0.093
0.9	$\pm$ 0.032
1.0	0.000

The c j c's on the development of the
soffit may be constructed by means of a
pattern, one side of which is cut by the
curve *k* O$_2$ *m*, and the other side is
straight and parallel to *l* X. By placing
this pattern upon the curve *k* O$_2$ *m*, lay-
ing a straight-edge along the back, and
then sliding the pattern till it passes
through the different points of division
on the line *n* o, the proper portion of the
pattern for each curve will be found.
For construction upon a very large scale
—as, for instance, upon a platform the
true size of the arch—this method would
be impracticable. The point of the curve
k O$_2$ *m* which passes through any point
of division on the curve *n* o may then be
found by calculation. Find by measurement or computation the value of *x* for the
point of division—*i. e.*, its distance from
the line D D$_2$; take this distance as a
fractional part of πr—*i. e.*, as a value of
n—and, substituting in equation (41),
find the corresponding value of *y ;* this
will be the constant *c* of equation (38).
Subtracting this from the ordinates

found from Table III. will give the ordinates of the curve measured from a line parallel to O_1 X through the point of division. It would also be desirable to determine the exact point in which any c j c cut the curve D_2 C_2. We can approximate very closely to this as follows: Find the point as nearly as possible by sketching in the curve from Table III.; through the point thus found draw a parallel to O_1 X; find the distance from this parallel to the one drawn through the point of division on n o corresponding to the same c j c; add this distance to the value of c found as above; take this as the value of y in equation (45), and compute from it the corresponding value of x; this will be the true abscissa of the curve on the line parallel to O_1 X through the point as first found, and of course will give the intersection of the c j c with the curve D_2 C_2 with great accuracy.

The h j s's are, of course, planes parallel to the P F. The c j s's are a species of conoid generated by a right line moving on the axis of the cylinder as one directrix, a c j c as another, and remaining always perpendicular to the former. Any plane perpendicular to the axis is therefore a plane directer. The intersection of any c j s with the P F will be a curve, several points of which will be needed in a construction upon a large scale. These may easily be found by drawing one or more semicircles between $D'V'C_1$ and $B'V'A_2$, finding, by Table III., the curves corresponding to I O L M, for the cylinders of which these semicircles are the vertical projections, and then erecting perpendiculars to the ground line from the points of intersection of these curves with the P F (or planes parallel to it) to meet the semicircles. Projected on a plane parallel to the P F, these curves of intersection of the c j s's with the P F will be normal to the elliptical section cut from the soffit by the P F at the points in which they cut it, and hence will be tangent to the projections on the same plane of the c j c's. All the above remarks apply also to the intersection of a c j s with any h j s—*i. e.*, any plane parallel to the P F.

In order to cut the voussoirs patterns must be made of the cylindrical and plane faces of each. It will also facilitate the operation to construct each in isometric projection, drawing on the cylindrical face one or more elements of the cylinder as guides in the cutting. Cut first the two plane faces of the voussoir precisely parallel to each other; cut roughly another plane face, making an angle with these two approximately equal to that between the P F and a tangent plane to the soffit at some point of the cylindrical face of the voussoir (*i. e.*, to the angle β of equation (51), from which equation its value may be found); lay the stone in such a position that the first two faces shall be vertical, and the third uppermost; apply to the vertical faces the patterns for the ends of the voussoir, with the edges next the soffit uppermost, their relative position being fixed by measurement from the drawings; mark out the ends by the patterns, and also the points where one or more elements of the cylinder pierces the h j s; sink drafts in the upper face connecting these points, and then cut the cylindrical face by a templet cut to the radius of the soffit, and applied at right angles to the elements. Next apply the pattern of the soffit, and draw by it the lines a b, c d, for the edges of the stone. In the figure a d is an element of

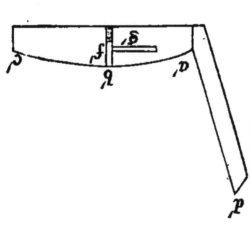

the cylinder, the stone being seen from above, and being taken from a course near the crown of the arch.

The warped faces can be cut by means of a templet of the form shown in the accompanying figure. The arc a b c » a' b' c' is cut to the radius of the cylinder, and the arm a d » a' d' is firmly fixed so as to be normal to the arc at the point

$a \gg a'$. The cross-bar $e f$ is perpendicular to $a c$, and its upper edge also perpendicu-

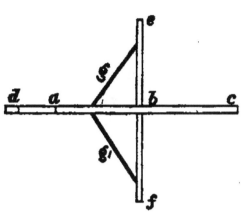

lar to the plane of $a\,b\,c \gg a'\,b'\,c'$ and $a\,d \gg a'\,d'$. $g \gg g'$ and $g_1 \gg g'$ are braces. Suppose the stone were cut, then, if the curved edge of the templet

were applied to the cylindrical face with the edge of cross-bar $e\,f$ coinciding with an element of the cylinder, and the point $a \gg a'$ at the edge of the voussoir, the edge $a\,d \gg a'\,d'$ of the normal arm would lie upon the warped face, and coincide with an element of it. If a number of drafts be sunk in the stone, then, by means of this templet, the warped faces can be easily cut. It only remains to cut the Ex s of the voussoir. If this surface is to be a cylinder concentric with the soffit, the intersections of this cylinder with the c j s's can be at once laid off on the stone by the aid of the templet. Measure on $a\,d\,\text{»}\,a'\,d'$ from $a'\,\text{»}\,a'$ the distance r_1-r, between soffit and Ex s; mark the point, and, applying the templet as described above, mark on the stone any number of points in the required curve. If the arch is to be built upon with stone, it would be better to cut the Ex s in steps, each stone having one or more horizontal and vertical plane faces when in position in the arch. \This would not add to the difficulty of *cutting* the stones, though it would somewhat to that of making the drawings. This way of cutting the stones is shown in the drawing of the arch according to the " cow's horn " method.

The diedral angle at the edge of a voussoir must not be less than a certain limit, otherwise the stone will be deficient in strength at this edge. The limit is usually taken at 60°; hence it follows that a *full centred* arch should not be constructed by this method with a greater obliquity than 60°; but, as the

angle between a tangent plane to the
soffit and the P F *increases* as the element of contact is taken higher above
the springing plane, up to 90° at the
crown, it is evident that a *segmental*
arch may be built with a greater obliquity than 60°, whose diedral angles
will be within the limits. To find the
chord of the segment (*i. e.*, the
span),

Let $\alpha = C_2 \, D_2 \, D' = $ obliquity of
arch.

Let $\beta = $ angle between P F and tangent plane to soffit; *i. e.*, its limiting
angle.

Let $\gamma = $ angle between the tangent
plane to soffit and the H P.

Then we have a right-angled spherical triangle, and by spherical trigonometry,
$$cos \; \beta = cos \; \alpha \; sin \; \gamma$$

$$\text{or } sin \; \gamma = \frac{cos \; \beta}{cos \; \alpha},$$

$$(51) \quad \therefore \text{Span} = 2 \, r \; sin \; \gamma = \frac{2 \, r \, cos \; \beta}{cos \; \alpha}$$

If we let $\beta = 60°$, then $\cos \beta = \frac{1}{2}$;

$$\therefore \quad \text{Span} = \frac{r}{\cos \alpha} = r \text{ secant } \alpha.$$

Also $\cos \alpha = \dfrac{r}{\text{span}}$ from which we can determine the limit of obliquity for a given segment.

If the span $= r$, then $\cos \alpha = 1$, and $\alpha = o$. Therefore we may give any obliquity to the arch that we please without passing the limit. If $\alpha = 30°$, the limiting span is

$$\text{Span} = \frac{2\,r}{\sqrt{3}} = 1.1546\,r.$$

The security of the arch constructed after this method will next be considered. In Fig. 2 the curves Q P' a and Q P$_1'$ b are the vertical projections of the curves cut from the o j s, whose directrices are the axis of the arch, O Q, and the curvé K O P$_1$ by the planes P c and P$_1$ O$_1$. These curves will be shown to have maximum points at P P' and P$_1$ P$_1'$ where they pierce the soffit. h K O L g is the horizontal projection of the curve cut from

the same c j's by the horizontal plane *ef,*
and it will be shown that its tangent at
the point of piercing the soffit is perpendicular to the P F. It will likewise be
shown that the tangent plane to the c j s
at any point of the c j c is perpendicular
to the tangent to the elliptical section
parallel to the P F at that point. Hence,
where it intersects the soffit every c j s is
exactly normal to that direction which
we have assumed to be the direction of
the pressure.

First to obtain the equation of a c j s.
Let the line O X be the axis of *x,* the line
Z O Q the axis of *z ;* then let the axis of
y be a vertical line through O. Then the
equations of the curve K O P P$_1$ will be

(*a*) $$x^2 + y^2 = r^2$$

(*b*) $$z = \frac{r^2}{h} \, l_0 \left(\frac{r-x}{r+x} \right).$$

Equation (*b*) is derived from equation
(44) by substituting *z* for *y* and changing
the sign of the right hand member, because the axis O Q in equation (44) was
considered as positive from O toward Q,

while now it is taken as positive from O toward Z.

Let $\dfrac{h}{r^2} = c$, and solve equation (b) for x.

$$\therefore e^{cs} = \frac{r - x}{r + x}; \text{ whence}$$

$$(52) \qquad x = r \cdot \frac{1 - e^{cs}}{1 + e^{cs}}$$

For the point x_1 we have

$$(53) \qquad x_1 = r \cdot \frac{1 - e^{cz}_1}{1 + e^{cs}_1}$$

Substitute value of x_1 from (53) in (a).

$$\therefore y_1^2 = r^2 - r^2 \cdot \frac{1 - 2 e^{cs}_1 + e^{2cs}_1}{1 + 2 e^{cs}_1 + e^{2cs}_1}$$

$$= r^2 \left(\frac{1 + 2 e^{cs}_1 + e^{2cs}_1 - 1 + 2 e^{cs}_1 - e^{2cs}_1}{(1 + e^{cs}_1)^2} \right)$$

$$(54) \qquad \therefore y_1 = \frac{2 r \sqrt{e^{cs}_1}}{1 + e^{cs}_1}$$

The equation of a line in X Y through the points $(x_1\, y_1)$ and $(x_2\, y_2)$ is

$$(55) \qquad \frac{y - y_2}{x - x_2} = \frac{y_1 - y_2}{x_1 - x_2}.$$

Since O Q is a directrix of the surface, we shall have

(56) $x_1 = y_1 = o$

∴ substituting from (53), (54), and (56) in (55)

$$\frac{y}{x} = \frac{2 r \sqrt{e^{\alpha_1}}}{1 + e^{\alpha_1}} \cdot \frac{1 + e^{\alpha_1}}{r(1 - e^{\alpha_1})};$$

or reducing and making z_1 general by dropping the subscript,

(57) $$\frac{y}{x} = \frac{2 e^{\frac{\alpha}{2}}}{1 - e^{\alpha}} = \frac{2 e^{\frac{hz}{r^2}}}{1 - e^{\frac{hz}{r^2}}},$$

which is the equation of a c j s.

Intersect this surface by the vertical plane P c d, whose equation is

(58) $$z = \frac{2 r}{h} (a_1 - x),$$

in which $a = O c =$ intercept on X, and

$$\frac{2 r}{h} = tan \; \alpha.$$

Substituting value of z from (58) in (57),

(59) $$\frac{y}{x} = \frac{2 e^{\frac{a_1 - x}{r}}}{1 - e^{\frac{2(a_1 - x)}{r}}} = \frac{2 e^{u}}{1 - e^{2u}}$$

if we let $u = \dfrac{a_1 - x}{r}.$

This is the equation of the curves Q P′ a, Q P$_1$′ b, etc. In (59) if $x = a_1$, $y = \infty$; ∴ the line $x = a_1$ is an asymptote. Also if $x = o$, $y = o$, and if $x = \pm\infty$, $y = o$, and the axis of x is an asymptote.

Differentiating (59)

$$\frac{dy}{dx} = \frac{2(1 - e^{2u})\left(e^u + xe^u\left(\dfrac{du}{dx}\right)\right) + 4\ e^{2u}\ x\left(\dfrac{du}{dx}\right)}{(1 - e^{2u})^2}$$

But $\dfrac{du}{dx} = -\dfrac{1}{r}$, therefore after reduction

$$(60) \quad \frac{dy}{dx} = 2\ e^u\left\{\frac{r - x - (r + x)e^{2u}}{r(1 - e^{2u})^2}\right\}$$

For a maximum $\dfrac{dy}{dx} = o$;

$$\therefore\quad r - x - (r + x)\ e^{2u} = o.$$

$$(61) \qquad e^{2u} = \frac{r - x}{r + x};$$

This equation gives the values of x for which y is a maximum.

Now eliminate y between equations (59) and (a),

$$\therefore \quad x^2 + \frac{4\, e^{2u}\, x^2}{(1-e^{2u})^2} = r^2; \text{ whence}$$

$$x^2 \left(\frac{1+e^{2u}}{1-e^{2u}}\right)^2 = r^2; \quad \text{therefore solving}$$

for e^{2u},

$$(61') \qquad e^{2u} = \frac{r-x}{r+x}.$$

This equation, which gives the x co-ordinate of the point of intersection of the curves Q P' a, Q P' b, etc., with the circle D' V C$_2$, is identical with (61), which gives x where y is a maximum; therefore the curve whose equations are

$$\begin{cases} y = \dfrac{2\, e^u\, x}{1-e^{2u}} \\[2ex] z = \dfrac{2\, r}{h}(a_1 - x) \end{cases}$$

has its tangent line horizontal at the point of piercing the soffit.

To find the inclination of the tangent at the point where the curve pierces a cylinder concentric with the soffit whose radius is r_1. If the co-ordinates of this point be x_1 y_1 we have by substituting in (61'), u_1 for u, r_1 for r, and x_1 for x,

$$e^{u_1} = \frac{r_1 - x_1}{r_1 + x_1}; \quad \therefore e^{u_1} = \sqrt{\frac{r_1 - x_1}{r_1 + x_1}}.$$

Substituting these values in (60),

$$\frac{dy_1}{dx_1} = \frac{2}{r} \sqrt{\frac{r_1 - x_1}{r_1 + x_1}} \left\{ \frac{r - x_1 - (r + x_1)\dfrac{r_1 - x_1}{r_1 + x_1}}{\left(1 - \dfrac{r_1 - x_1}{r_1 + x_1}\right)^2} \right\}$$

whence by reduction,

$$(62) \quad \frac{dy_1}{dx_1} = \frac{(r - r_1)\sqrt{r_1^2 - x_1^2}}{r\,x_1} = -\frac{\delta y_1}{r\,x_1},$$

if we let $r_1 - r = \delta$.

If we multiply $\dfrac{dy_1}{dx_1}$ by $\cos \alpha$, we obtain the tangent of the angle between the tangent line to the curves c P » Q P′a, O_1 P$_1$ » Q P$_1'b$, etc., at the point of pierc-

ing the Ex s and the H P. Call this
angle t, then

$$(63) \qquad \tan t = - \frac{\delta y_1 \cos \alpha}{r \, x_1}.$$

Suppose $\alpha = 60°$, $\dfrac{\delta}{r} = \dfrac{2}{15}$, then

If $x_1 = r_1 \cos 10°$, $y_1 = r_1 \sin 10°$, and $t = 0° \, 40' \, 20''$
" $x_1 = r_1 \cos 20°$, $y_1 = r_1 \sin 20°$, and $t = 1° \, 23' \, 20''$
" $x_1 = r_1 \cos 30°$, $y_1 = r_1 \sin 30°$, and $t = 2° \, 12' \, 15''$

Intersect the locus of equation (57) by
the plane

$$y = b;$$

$$\therefore \quad \frac{b}{x} = \frac{2 \, e^{\frac{cz}{2}}}{1 - e^{cz}};$$

$$\therefore \quad b \, e^{cz} + 2 \, x \, e^{\frac{cz}{2}} - b = 0;$$

solving this for $e^{\frac{cz}{2}}$ as a quadratic,

$$e^{\frac{cz}{2}} = \frac{-x \pm \cdot \sqrt{x^2 + b^2}}{b}$$

$$(64) \quad \therefore \quad z = \frac{2}{c} \, l_e \left(\frac{-x \pm \sqrt{x^2 + b^2}}{b} \right).$$

Differentiating and reducing,

(65) $\dfrac{dz}{dx} = \dfrac{2}{\mp c \sqrt{x^2 + b^2}} = \dfrac{2\,r^2}{\mp h \sqrt{x^2 + b^2}}$

When $x = 0, \dfrac{dz_0}{dx_0} = \mp \dfrac{2r^2}{bh} = \mp \dfrac{r}{b} \tan \alpha.$

" $b = r_1$ and $x = 0, \dfrac{dz_{or_1}}{dx_{or_1}} = \dfrac{2r}{h} \cdot \dfrac{r}{r_1} = \dfrac{r}{r_1} \tan \alpha$

To find the angle at which the locus of
(64) pierces a cylinder concentric with
the soffit, eliminate y between $y = b$ and
$x^2 + y^2 = r_1^2$.

$$\therefore \quad x_1^2 = r_1^2 - b^2.$$

Substitute this value of x in (65),

(66)

$$\therefore \dfrac{dz_1}{dx} = \dfrac{2\,r^2}{\mp h \sqrt{r_1^2 - b^2 + b^2}} = \mp \dfrac{2\,r}{h} \cdot \dfrac{r}{r_1} = \dfrac{r}{r_1} \tan \alpha$$

If $r_1 = r, \dfrac{dz_1}{dx_1} = \tan \alpha.$ We see there-

fore that the locus of (64) pierces the soffit at the angle α.—i. e., its tangent is
there perpendicular to the P F—and that
it pierces any cylinder concentric with

the soffit at a constant angle for **any** given value of α, no matter what value b may have.

The surface is thus seen to differ very essentially from the helicoid previously considered, as regards tendency to sliding on the coursing joints, as is indeed evident from a comparison of the two drawings.

The tangent plane to the c j s at any point of the c j c, as P P', must contain the element of the surface through the point and the tangent line at the point to the curve cut out by a horizontal plane through the point; therefore it must be perpendicular to the P F. The tang. of the angle between it and the H P will be equal to

(67) $tan \; 'P \; Q \; C_2 \; cosec \; \alpha = tan \; N$

if N be the angle between the normal at P P' and a vertical line; but this is also the expression for the tangent of the angle between a vertical line and the tangent line at P P' to the elliptical section of the soffit parallel to the P F; therefore the assumed direction of pressure is normal

to the c j s at any point of the c j c.
This result might have been predicted
from the mode of construction of the c j c's.
The curve cut from a c j s by the plane

$$(68) \qquad z = \frac{h}{2r}(x - a_1)$$

parallel to the P F is always convex towards the springing plane between the
soffit and Ex s. Its equation found by
substitution in (57) is

$$(69) \qquad \frac{y}{x} = \frac{2\,e^{\frac{h^2}{4r^2}(x-a^1)}}{1-e^{\frac{h^2}{2r^2}(x-a^1)}} = \frac{2\,e^v}{1-e^{2v}}$$

if we place $\dfrac{h^2}{4r^2}(x - a_1) = v.$

By differentiation and reduction we obtain
in the same way in which we found (62)

$$(70) \qquad \frac{dy_1}{dx_1} = \frac{y_1}{x_1}\left(\frac{4\,r^2 + h^2\,r_1}{4\,r^2}\right),$$

which is the tangent of the angle between
the tangent line to the locus of (69) at
point of piercing the cylinder whose ra-

dius is r_1 and the horizontal plane. To obtain the angle between the tangent line to the curve in space whose equations are (68) and (69) and the H P, multiply (70)

by sin $\alpha = \dfrac{2r}{\sqrt{h^2 + 4 r^2}}$

Call this angle t_1, then

$$(71) \quad \tan t_1 = \frac{y_1}{x_1}\left(\frac{4 r^3 + h^2 r_1}{2 r^2 \sqrt{h^2 + 4 r^2}}\right) =$$

$$\frac{y_1}{x_1} \cdot \frac{r \sin^2 a + r_1 \cos^2 \alpha}{r \sin \alpha}$$

If $r_1 = r$, which gives the point of piercing the soffit,

$$(72) \ \tan t_s = \frac{y_1}{x_1} \cdot \frac{\sqrt{4 r^2 + h^2}}{2 r} = \frac{y_1}{x_1} \cosec \alpha,$$

which is identical with equation (67).

If $\dfrac{r_1}{r} = \dfrac{17}{15}$, and $\alpha = 60°$, then

when $\dfrac{y_1}{x_1} = \tan 10°$, $t_1 = 11° 52' 50''$, $t_s = 11° 30' 30''$

" $\dfrac{y_1}{x_1} = \tan 20°$, $t_1 = 23° 28' 16''$, $t_s = 22° 47' 45''$

" $\dfrac{y_1}{x_1} = \tan 30°$, $t_1 = 34° 33' 30''$, $t_s = 33° 41' 24''$

, The points for which t_1 and t_2 are found being on the same radius are of course on different curves, though these curves are so near together that the difference between the angles t_1 and t_2 is very nearly the same as the difference between the slope of the tangents to a single curve at the points of piercing the soffit and Ex s.

The function $n = t_1 - t_2$ is found by differentiation to be a maximum when

$$\frac{y_1}{x_1} = \frac{1}{\sqrt{\sin^2 \alpha + \frac{r_1}{r} \cos^2}} = tan \ 44° \ 32'$$

where α and $\frac{r_1}{r}$ have the values assigned above. The maximum value of the function in this case is $t_1 - t_2 = 55' \ 31''$.

It appears, therefore, that at *no* point on the c j s, between the soffit and the Ex s does the normal to the c j s vary to any extent from the assumed direction of pressure.

COW'S HORN METHOD.

In this method the soffit is a warped surface called the *Corne de Vache*, or Cow's Horn, generated in the following manner. A right line moves on three directrices, which are : 1st, two equal ellipses in parallel, vertical planes, having their transverse axes in the springing plane of the arch; and 2d, a right line drawn in the springing plane perpendicular to the plane of the ellipses, through the centre of the parallelogram formed by joining the extremities of the transverse axes of the ellipses. These ellipses may, of course, as a particular case, be circles. In Fig. 3, the plane of one face of the arch is taken as the V P, and the springing plane is the H P. In referring to Fig. 3, the following notation will be employed. Any letter with h written above it as an exponent, means the *horizontal* projection of a point, and the same letter, with exponent v, is the *vertical* projection of the same point, and this point will be referred to as the point A, B, etc.; *i.e.*, the point whose projections are A^h A^v, B^h B^v, etc. A line drawn through these two points would be, therefore, the line A B. If one projection of a point is in the ground line, h or

v, as the case may be, is replaced by o, and if the point itself is in the ground line, it will be designated by the letter alone without exponent.

In Fig. 3, the parallelogram $A^h B^h C D$ is the horizontal projection of the soffit. Its centre O is the point through which the rectilinear directrix of the soffit is drawn perpendicular to the V P, since this coincides with a P F. The three directrices of the cow's horn surface are then the ellipses D S I C, and A K N B, and the right line O Z lying in the H P. The elements of the surface are to be drawn so as to cut these three directrices. The vertical projection of O Z is a point in the ground line at O^o, hence the vertical projections of the elements will be lines radiating from this point. By dropping perpendiculars from the points where the vertical projections of the elements meet the vertical projections of the elliptical directrices to the horizontal projections of the same, the horizontal projections of the elements will be found, as will be seen in the case of the elements

R S, P Q, etc. *The elements of the surface are the edges of the voussoirs*—that is,
the c j c's, which, therefore, in this method
become right lines, while the h j c's, being
sections of the soffit parallel to the P F,
are curves of the 4th degree. It is, of
course, impossible to *develop* the soffit,
since the consecutive elements are not in
the same plane.

The arch must be divided up into
courses on the *median section* in order
that the two faces may be alike. To find
this, draw the vertical projections of a
number of elements, and bisect the portion of each included between the points
in which it cuts the vertical projections
of the elliptical directrices; through
these points of bisection the median
curve may be drawn. In Fig. 3, it is the
line L T, and is only drawn as far as the
crown of the arch. The length of this
median curve would have to be ascer-
tained by construction upon a large scale,
and accurate measurement. It may then
be divided into a convenient odd number of equal parts, and the elements of

the surface, which are the c j c's drawn through the points of division.

The h j s's in this method, are planes parallel to the planes of the faces of the arch, while the c j s's are hyperbolic paraboloids the method of whose construction will next be shown. It will first be shown that a hyperbolic paraboloid may be drawn having an element in common with any warped surface, and normal to this surface at every point of the common element. It is proved in works on descriptive geometry, that, if two warped surfaces have a common element, and have common tangent planes at three different points of this element, they are tangent to each other throughout the length of this element. Therefore, we can always draw a hyperbolic paraboloid *tangent* to a warped surface along an element; for draw tangent planes at three points of any element, and in these planes, through the points of tangency, draw right lines parallel to some given plane; if a rectilinear generatrix be moved on these lines, a hyperbolic para-

boloid will be generated tangent to the
warped surface along the element. Now,
revolve this tangent surface about the
common element as an axis through an
angle of 90°; it will then be normal to
the other surface at every point of the
element. If the lines drawn in the tangent planes are *perpendicular* to the common element, after revolution through
90°, they will be perpendicular to the
tangent planes, and hence normals to the
warped surface. Hence it follows that
the directrices for a c j s may be three
normals to the soffit, drawn at any convenient points of the corresponding c j′ c,
or element. The points at which normals
are most easily constructed are those in
which the element cuts the three directrices, but as the intersection with the
rectilinear directrix will generally be beyond the limits of the drawing, some
other point must be used instead of this
one. A method will now be given by
which a tangent line can be easily and
simply constructed at any point of any
section of the cow's horn surface, by a

plane parallel to the elliptical directrices.
This tangent line being found, of course
the normal to the surface at the point of

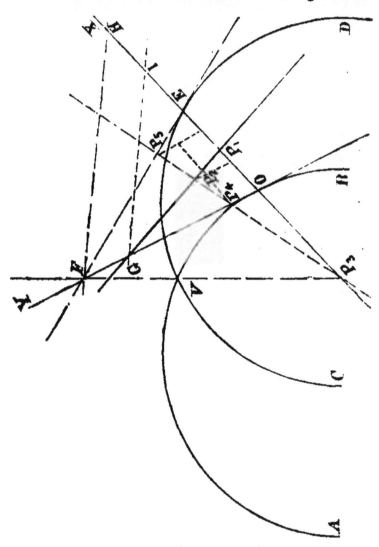

tangency can be drawn at once. Let
A V B and C V D be vertical projections

of the elliptical directrices, P_2 that of the rectilinear directrix, P_2 X that of the element through P_1, which is a point of some section of the soffit by a plane parallel to the P F, and O F and E F tangents to the curves A V B and C V D, at the points where they are cut by P_2 X. E F and O F will meet on P_2 F because this is the axis radical of the two curves.

Let O E $= a$, O F $= b$, P_2 O $= a_1$ and O $P_4 = b_1$. Take O as the origin of co-ordinates, the line P_2 X as the axis of abscissas, and the line O Y as the axis of ordinates. Then the equation of the tangent line E F will be

$$(72) \qquad \frac{x}{a} + \frac{y}{b} = 1;$$

that of the line P_2 P_5,

$$(73) \qquad \frac{x}{-a_1} + \frac{y}{b_1} = 1;$$

and that of the tangent line O F,

$$(74) \qquad x = 0.$$

We will now find the equation of the line cutting O X and P_2 P_5 in such a manner that $\dfrac{O\,P_1}{P_1\,E} = \dfrac{P_4\,P_2}{P_2\,P_5}$. Let O $P_1 =$

$n \times OE = n\,a.$ To find the co-ordinates of the point P_5 eliminate between (72) and (73)

$$\therefore\ y_5 = b - \frac{b}{a}\,x_5 = b_1 + \frac{b_1}{a_1}\,x_5$$

$$x_5 = \frac{a\,a_1\,(b - b_1)}{a_1\,b + a\,b_1},\ \text{similarly}$$

$$y_5 = \frac{b\,b_1\,(a + a_1)}{a_1\,b + a\,b_1}.$$

For the point P_4 the co-ordinates are

$$x_4 = 0, \qquad y_4 = b_1$$

Hence for P_2 we shall have

$$x_2 = n\,x_5 = \frac{n\,a\,a_1\,(b - b_1)}{a_1\,b + a\,b_1}$$

$$y_2 = b_1 + n(y_5 - b_1) = \frac{b_1(a_1\,b + a\,b_1 - na(b_1 - b))}{a_1\,b + a\,b_1};$$

and for P_1, $x_1 = n\,a$, $y_1 = 0$.

Substituting these values of $x_1\,y_1, x_2\,y_2$ in the equation of a line through two points

$$(y - y_1)\,(x_1 - x_2) = (x - x_1)\,(y_1 - y_2)$$

we have after reduction,

$$(75)\quad y = \frac{(n\,a - x)(a_1\,b + a\,b_1 - n\,a(b_1 - b))}{n\,a\,(a + a_1)}$$

which is the required line.

Now in this equation we may give to b_1 any value we please, positive or negative; suppose it to change gradually in value from some positive quantity to some negative, the line G P_1 will change position accordingly, and at the instant in which b_1 passes through zero it will be tangent to the section through P_1; for the law of this curve of section is, that it cuts off an nth part of the portion of any radial line included between the two curves A V B and C V D; hence at the instant that $b_1 = 0$ the line G P_1 coincides with an element of the curve. In the figure G P_1 is this limiting case; *i. e.*, the tangent at P_1, and the line of equation (75) would cut the axis of y very slightly nearer to F, but the two lines would so nearly coincide for this position of P_a P_b, that G P_1 is made to answer for both. Now in equation (75) make $b_1 = 0$ and we have the equation of the tang. to the curve of section.

$$(76) \quad \therefore \quad y = \frac{b\,(n\,a - x)\,(a_1 + n\,a)}{n\,a\,(a + a_1)}$$

For the intercept on Y let $x = 0$,

$$(77) \quad \therefore \quad y_0 = \frac{b \, (a_1 + n \, u)}{a + a_1}$$

or putting it into the form of a proportion,

$$(78) \quad a + a_1 : n \, a + a_1 :: b : y_0.$$

Hence to draw a tangent at any point of a curve of section of a cow's horn surface by a plane parallel to the curve directrices, draw the vertical projection of the element through the point (V P supposed parallel to P F), and tangents to the curved directrices at their points of intersection with the element; lay off E H and P_1 I each equal to P_2 O $= a_1$; draw H F to the point of intersection of the tangents previously drawn, and I G parallel to H F; through G draw G P_1, then will G P_1 be the required tangent line; for

$$\text{O H} = \text{O E} + \text{E H} = a + a_1,$$
$$\text{O I} = \text{O} P_1 + P_1 \text{ I} = n \, a + a_1,$$

and O F $= b$; $\therefore$ by (78) O G $= y_0$

We will now construct a hyperbolic paraboloid normal to the soffit, and intersecting it in the element R S. Since lines perpendicular to each other have

their projections on a plane parallel to
one of them perpendicular, the vertical
projections of the normals can be drawn
at once perpendicular to the tangents to
the vertical projections of the curve directrices and the median section at the
points R, U, and S. Their horizontal
projections will be perpendicular to the
horizontal traces of the tangent planes to
the soffit at R, U, and S. These tangent
planes will of course be the planes
through the tangent lines to the soffit
at R, U, and S, already drawn, and the
element of the surface R S. Portions
of their horizontal traces are $\alpha\beta$, $\gamma\delta$, and
$\epsilon\zeta$, to which the horizontal projections of
the normals S a, U b, and R c are perpendicular. These three normals are the
directrices of our c j s. To find an element of the 1st generation, pass a plane
through one directrix and find the points
where the other two pierce it; join these
points by a right line; this line will be
an element of the surface. Take, for
convenience, the plane which projects
a S on the vertical plane of projection,

then b and c will be the points in which the other directrices pierce this plane; therefore a c is an element of the first generation. Any number of other elements may now be found by merely dividing up a c and S R, or a S and c R proportionally, as in Fig. 3. In the figure the horizontal projections of several elements of each generation are drawn, but the vertical projections of those of the first generation only.

Next the intersections of the c ɟ s with the P F's and with the Ex s must be found. The vertical projection of the intersection of the c ɟ s just constructed with the V P is the line η S^r, of which the portion drawn varies but little from a right line. There are a number of forms in which the Ex s may be cut. It may be a cylinder whose axis passes through O and is parallel to E H; or a co-axial cow's horn surface generated on the extradosal ellipses H I_1 G and E K_1 F; or the exterior surface of each course may be cut like the course M_1 Q_1 by one vertical plane through f and k, and one

inclined through d, f_0 g and k; or each
course may be cut in a series of steps,
as in the course P N, by a number of
horizontal and vertical planes. The last
method would be preferable for the voussoirs at the ends of each course, however the others were cut.

Except in the case where the Ex s is
cylindrical, no face of a voussoir can be
cut by the aid of a templet. Cut first
two plane faces on the stone precisely
parallel for the ends of the voussoir. If
the Ex s is to be cut in the manner of
P N or P_1 N_1, it would be best to cut
next the other plane faces of the voussoir of which patterns can be made
from the drawings. Then apply the
patterns of the heads and mark the lines
on the stone, marking also the points
where one or more elements of the ruled
surfaces forming the soffit and c j s's
pierce the plane of the head of the voussoir. The warped faces can then be cut
by a straight edge. The soffit face
should be cut first, and the elements
forming the edges of the voussoir mark-

ed; then all the bounding lines of the coursing joint faces will be given on the stone, and draughts can be sunk by a straight-edge in a direction perpendicular to the soffit edges of the stone by which the c j s's may be cut.

The curves k^o l m and n o p are the evolutes of the ellipses A K B and D I C, and are convenient in drawing the normals to these curves which are required.

The curved directrices of this arch we take elliptical so as to correspond with the curves cut from the soffit in the other methods by planes parallel to the P F.

In each of the drawings the direct span is 30 ft., the oblique 34.64 ft. $\alpha = 60^\circ$, and the number of courses is 49.

It is evident from the drawing that if a perpendicular to the H P be erected at the point O, it will pierce the soffit in the line K I, which is parallel to the rectilinear directrix and lower than the highest points of the elliptical directrices, so that the crown of the arch curves downward toward the middle, from which peculiarity the surface derives its name, " cow's horn." Plainly, if this curvature were so great as to cause the median section of the soffit to be convex toward the springing plane at the crown, the arch would be unsafe; indeed, could not stand at all. We will investigate the conditions under which this will be the case, and to this end will obtain the equation of the surface. Let the line O X be the axis of X, O Z the axis of Z, and let the axis of Y be a vertical line through the origin O. The equations of the three directrices will then be

$$(79) \quad \begin{cases} \dfrac{(x+\varepsilon)^2}{a^2}+\dfrac{y^2}{b^2}=1 \\[2mm] (80) \quad z=-\delta \end{cases} \left.\right\} \begin{array}{c}\text{Equations of}\\ \text{D I C;}\end{array}$$

$$(81) \quad \begin{cases} \dfrac{(x-\varepsilon)^2}{a^2}+\dfrac{y^2}{b^2}+1 \\[2mm] (82) \quad z=\delta \end{cases} \left.\right\} \begin{array}{c}\text{Equations of}\\ \text{A K B;}\end{array}$$

(83) $x = 0, y = 0,$ equation of OZ; in which $\varepsilon = O°q = O°r$, and

$$\delta = OK = OI = \tfrac{1}{2} \text{ distance between the faces of the arch.}$$

The equation of a plane through the axis of z is

(84)
$$y = m x$$

in which $m = $ tangent of angle between plane and H P.

We will now find, by elimination, the co-ordinates of the points in which (79) and (81) pierce this plane, obtain the equations of the element through these points, and then eliminate the constant m. From (79) and (84) we obtain after reduction, and placing $a^2 m^2 + b^2 = k^2$,

$$x_1 = b \left[\frac{- b \varepsilon \pm a \sqrt{k^2 - \varepsilon^2 m^2}}{k^2} \right].$$

Similarly from (81) and (84),

$$x_2 = b \left[\frac{+ b \varepsilon \pm a \sqrt{k^2 - \varepsilon^2 m^2}}{k^2} \right].$$

Also from (80) and (82) we have

$$z_1 = - \delta \text{ and } z_2 = + \delta.$$

Substituting these values of x_1, x_2, z_1, and

z_2 in the equation $\dfrac{z - z_1}{x - x_1} = \dfrac{z_2 - z_1}{x_2 - x_1}$ of a line through two points in X Z, we have

$$(z+\delta)\frac{2b^2\varepsilon}{k^2} = 2\delta\left(x - \frac{-b^2\varepsilon \pm ab\sqrt{k^2-\varepsilon^2 m^2}}{k^2}\right)$$

and by reduction

(85) $\qquad b^2\,\varepsilon\,z - a^2\,\delta\,m^2\,x - \delta\,b^2\,x$
$$= a\,b\,\delta\,\sqrt{a^2\,m^2 + b^2 - \varepsilon^2\,m^2}$$

which is one equation of the element through $(x_1\ z_1)$ and $(x_2\ z_2)$, equation (84) being another.

Squaring (85), introducing the value of m from (84), and reducing, we obtain

$$\delta^2\left(\frac{x^2}{a^2}+\frac{y^2}{b^2}\right)^2 - \frac{2\,\delta\,\varepsilon\,x\,z}{a^2}\left(\frac{x^2}{a^2}+\frac{y^2}{b^2}\right) -$$

$$\delta^2\left(\frac{x^2}{a^2}+\frac{y^2}{b^2}\right) + \varepsilon^2\left(\frac{x^2 z^2}{a^4}+\frac{\delta^2 y^2}{a^2 b^2}\right) = 0;$$

or factoring,

$$(86)\,\delta\left\{\left(\frac{x^2}{a^2}+\frac{y^2}{b^2}\right)\delta - \frac{2\,\varepsilon\,x\,z}{a^2} - \delta\right\}\left(\frac{x^2}{a^2}+\frac{y^2}{b^2}\right)$$

$$+ \varepsilon^2\left(\frac{x^2 z^2}{a^4}+\frac{\delta^2 y^2}{a^2 b^2}\right) = 0$$

which is the equation of the cow's horn surface. If ε be taken negative, the obliquity of the arch will be in the opposite direction from that of Fig. 3.

Equation (86) contains only even powers of y, hence the surface is symmetrical with respect to the plane X Z.

If $z = \pm \delta$, it becomes

$$\frac{(x \mp \varepsilon)^2}{a^2} + \frac{y^2}{b^2} = 1,$$

the equations of the curved directrices.

If $x = 0$, we have $y = \pm b\sqrt{1 - \frac{\varepsilon^2}{a^2}}$, two

right lines parallel to the rectilinear directrix.

If $y = 0$, then $z = \dfrac{\delta(x \mp a)}{\varepsilon}$.

If $z =$ some constant $= n\,\delta$, we have the intersection by a plane parallel to the P F.

$$(87) \quad \left\{\frac{x^2}{a^2} + \frac{y^2}{b^2} - \frac{2\,\varepsilon\,n\,x}{a^2} - 1\right\}\left(\frac{x^2}{a^2} + \frac{y^2}{b^2}\right)$$

$$+ \varepsilon^2\left(\frac{n^2\,x^2}{a^4} + \frac{y^2}{a^2\,b^2}\right) = 0;$$

and if $n = 0$, this becomes

$$(88) \quad \left(\frac{x^2}{a^2} + \frac{y^2}{b^2}\right)^2 - \frac{x^2}{a^2} - \left(1 - \frac{\varepsilon^2}{a^2}\right)\frac{y^2}{b^2} = 0;$$

the equation of the median section.

In (88) let $y = b\sqrt{1 - \frac{\varepsilon^2}{a^2}}$ = height above X Z of lowest point of crown of arch = ordinate of median section where $x = 0$.

$$\therefore \left(\frac{x^2}{a^2} + \left(1 - \frac{\varepsilon^2}{a^2}\right)\right)^2 - \frac{x^2}{a^2} - \left(1 - \frac{\varepsilon^2}{a^2}\right)^2 = 0;$$

whence by reduction

$$(89) \quad x = \pm \sqrt{2\,\varepsilon^2 - a^2}.$$

This equation gives the x co-ordinates of the points in which a tangent to the median section at the extremity of its minor axis cuts the curve. In order that the arch may stand, these points must be imaginary.

In (89) when $\varepsilon > a\sqrt{\tfrac{1}{2}} > 0.7071\,a$, x is real;

  " $\varepsilon = a\sqrt{\tfrac{1}{2}} = 0.7071\,a$, $x = 0$;

  " $\varepsilon < a\sqrt{\tfrac{1}{2}} < 0.7071\,a$, x is imaginary.

The third of these cases is therefore the condition of stability.

The same result may be obtained by differentiating (88), placing $\dfrac{dy}{dx} = 0$, and making the condition that there shall be only one value of x for which y is a maximum.

In equation (86) if $\varepsilon = 0$, we have

$$\frac{x^2}{a^2} + \frac{y^2}{b^2} = 1,$$

a cylinder whose axis is O Z.

If $\varepsilon = a$, by transposing and extracting square root

$$\delta\left(\frac{x^2}{a^2} + \frac{y^2}{b^2}\right) - \frac{x\,z}{a} = \pm\,\frac{\delta\,x}{a},$$

the equation of two cones tangent to each other along the axis of z.

The equations of the c j s's can be found without difficulty, but they contain so many constants and are so complex as to be of no practical utility. The character of the arch as regards stability and tendency to sliding on the coursing joints, can be easily seen by examination of Fig. 3 and comparing it with Figs. 1 and 2. It will be noticed that the vertical projection of each element takes a direction between those of the normals to the elliptical directrices at the points where it cuts them; therefore at some point between these it must coincide with the vertical projection of the normal to the section at that point by the heading plane through it. It follows that at this point the element will be perpendicular to the direction which has been assumed to be that of the pressure, and from the manner of its construction the c j s will be also normal to this direction. At the crown this point is midway between the faces of the arch, and as we approach the springing plane it moves toward the points A and C. The curve λ U ϑ is cut from the c j s, R S *a c* by a horizontal plane through the point U, and the portion of it from U toward ϑ which would lie upon the coursing joint would evidently be nearly perpendicular to the direction of pressure. The curve μ ν ξ is cut from the coursing joint surface through the element M N, and the portion which is upon the voussoir is almost exactly perpendicular to the P F. $\mu_1\,\nu_1\,\xi_1$ is cut from the surface of the lower face of the same course M Q. $\pi\,\rho\,\varsigma$ is the curve cut from the c j s through the first c j c on that side by a vertical plane perpendicular to the P F through B. It varies but slightly in the distance $\pi\,\varsigma$ from a right line. $\pi_1\,\rho_1\varsigma_1$ is a similar curve cut by a plane through L. The first one or two c j s's from the springing plane vary so slightly from a plane in the portion included between the inner and outer surfaces of the arch that they might well enough be made *exactly* plane when the number of courses is large.

This method of constructing the arch gives results therefore, as regards tendency to sliding in the coursing joints, *intermediate* between those found in the two methods previously considered, but approaching far more nearly to those obtained in the logarithmic method; that is, the c j s's are nearly normal to the direction of pressure.

An arch may also be constructed with the cow's horn soffit and *plane* coursing joints as follows : On any element, as M N, take points midway between the heading planes, and at these points draw normals to the surface; through these normals and the element pass planes which will form the c j s's. The coursing joint will then be cut in a series of steps, and a portion of the voussoirs will have a triangular vertical face midway between the two ends. If the Ex s be also cut in steps, the voussoirs will have all their faces plane except the soffit, and all their edges straight lines except the intersections of the heading planes with the soffit. The construction of the drawings and cutting of the stones would thus be comparatively easy.

What was said in treating of the logarithmic method with regard to the limit of obliquity by reason of the edges of the voussoirs becoming too sharp where α is less than 60°, applies equally well to this method of construction. In this case, however, as in that, *segmental* arches can be built in which $\alpha < 60°$. Equation (51′) could be used to ascertain

approximately the allowable span for a
given radius and obliquity when the
semi-axes of the elliptical directrices have

the ratio to each other $\dfrac{b}{a} = \cos. \alpha$; that

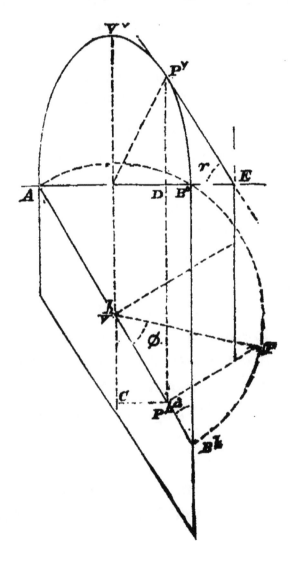

is, such that if the soffit were cylindrical, its right section would be a circle.

If the curved directrices are circles, we may obtain an approximate result as follows, by supposing the soffit to be cylindrical.

Let the angle $P_1V^hP^h = \Phi,$

" $P^vED = \gamma,$

" $AB^hB^\circ = \alpha,$

the distance $CP^h = x_1,$

" $DP^v = y_1$

and $\beta =$ the angle between the P F and the tangent plane to the soffit (supposed cylindrical).

A $V^v B^\circ$ will then be a right section of the cylinder, and its equation will be, if $V^h P = r,$

$$\frac{x^2}{r^2 \sin^2 \alpha} + \frac{y^2}{r^2} = 1.$$

The equation of the tangent plane to the cylinder will then be

$$\frac{x\,x_1}{r^2 \sin^2 \alpha} + \frac{yy_1}{r^2} = 1$$

or $$y = \frac{r^2}{y_1} - \frac{x_1}{y_1 \sin^2 \alpha} \cdot x$$

$\therefore$ $\tan \gamma = \dfrac{x_1}{y_1 \sin^2 \alpha},$ and

$$\sin \gamma = \frac{x_1}{\sqrt{x_1^2 + y_1^2 \sin^4 \alpha}}.$$

But by (51) $\sin \gamma = \dfrac{\cos \beta}{\cos \alpha} = \dfrac{1}{2 \cos \alpha}$ if we let $\beta = 60°$.

$$\therefore \quad \frac{x_1}{\sqrt{x_1^2 + y_1^2 \sin^4 \alpha}} = \frac{1}{2 \cos \alpha}$$

$$\therefore \quad 4 x^2 \cos^2 \alpha = x_1^2 + y_1^2 \sin^4 \alpha.$$

Dividing by x_1^2,

$$4 \cos^2 \alpha = 1 + \frac{y_1^2}{x_1^2} \sin^4 \alpha.$$

We have $\tan. \Phi = \dfrac{y_1}{x_1 \operatorname{cosec} \alpha}$, whence

$$\frac{y_1^2}{x_1^2} = \tan^2 \Phi \operatorname{cosec}^2 \alpha.$$

Substituting

$$4 \cos^2 \alpha - 1 = \tan^2 \Phi \sin^2 \alpha$$

$$\therefore \quad \tan \Phi = \frac{\sqrt{4 \cos^2 \alpha - 1}}{\sin \alpha} \quad \text{whence}$$

$$\cos \Phi = \frac{\tan \alpha}{\sqrt{3}}.$$

(90) Oblique span $= 2\,r\,cos\,\Phi$

$$= \frac{2}{\sqrt{3}} r\, tan\, \alpha = 2\,r.\,\frac{tan\,\alpha}{tan\,60^{b}}.$$

If α 30°, oblique span $= \frac{2}{3} r.$

If $\alpha = 45°$, oblique span $= \frac{2}{\sqrt{3}} r = 1.1547\,r$

In the cow's horn soffit this formula, as well as (51′), will make the diedral angles at the edges of the voussoirs in the first course slightly greater or less than 60°, according to their position in the course. The exact solution of the problem involves an equation of the 4th degree with four real roots.

COMPARISON OF THE THREE METHODS.

There is one advantage possessed by the helicoidal method over each of the others; viz., that it may be constructed of brick. This is owing to the fact that the successive c j c's are *parallel*, so that the voussoirs, except those at the ends of the courses, are all exactly alike, while in the other methods each stone is different from the next one, though the *two halves* of the arch on each side of the keystone are alike, so that any stone cut for one side will fit also in the corresponding place on the other side. The fact that the different voussoirs are alike in the helicoidal method, of course lessens the labor of preparing the drawings, and of making the necessary measurements. As regards the difficulty of *cutting* the stones, however, this method does not seem to have any serious advantage over the others even by the approximate method of cutting which has been mentioned, while if the coursing and heading joint faces were cut with exactness, as *helicoids*, the difficulty would be fully equal to if not greater than that by the other methods.

It may be considered an advantage as regards *appearance* that the quoin-stones should be all alike, or rather those faces of the quoin-stones which coincide with the faces of the arch. This, of course, is the case only with the helicoidal method.

It appears to me, however, that the gradual decrease in the size of these faces from one side of the arch to the other would not be displeasing to the eye, when taken in connection with the direction of the c j c's which would make the *reason* for the decrease obvious. The real test, however, of the relative value of the different methods would appear to be that of *security*. When this test is applied, the logarithmic and cow's horn methods both excel by far the helicoidal. It has been shown that in the last mentioned, when semi-circular, there is *always* a tendency to sliding on the coursing joints, both above and below a certain point; that is, the assumed direction of pressure is nowhere normal to the coursing joints except at a certain height above the springing plane equal to r sin. $39° \, 32' \, 23''$, and that near the springing-plane this tendency to sliding increases rapidly with the obliquity up to $\alpha = 20°$ (about); while in the logarithmic method along each c j c this tendency is zero; that is, the assumed direction of pressure is normal to the c j s at any point of the c j c, and in the cow's horn the tendency is small as compared with the helicoidal.

The logarithmic method, therefore, seems to approximate to theoretical perfection as regards security, is followed closely by the cow's horn, and at a great distance by the helicoidal.

The cow's horn soffit admits of plane coursing-joints, as has been shown, which are not feasible in the others, and thus possesses an advantage over them, if such an approximate construction be desirable. If *cheapness* be an important item to be considered, the last-mentioned method would seem to present most advantages, as avoiding almost entirely the use of curved surfaces, and at the same time reducing the sliding tendency to a small amount.

If the main thing to be considered is *security*, the logarithmic method must stand first.

Milton Keynes UK
Ingram Content Group UK Ltd.
UKHW040930180224
437992UK00003B/151

9 783385 251496